BILBO THE CLOWN FIGHTS EVIL

BY
T. THORNTON GRAY

This story it dedicated to my family. Without whom, it would not exist. It was first glimpsed in the flames of a campfire, through the wonder and laughter of a summer night. The people we cherish, make the times we cherish. And I cherish you so much. I Love you, Nicole, Dustin, and Rebecca.

It's hard to tell what circumstances put a man where he ends up. Some men are meant for greatness, most are not. William Bozwick's one true love thought "not" when she left him for, well, anyone better. It wasn't because he didn't try. No one could say he didn't try. Nothing ever meant more to him. Turns out trying doesn't always work out. He tried hard. Worked hard. But William was a hard worker at all he did. He spent twenty-five years of hard work helping his boss and one-time friend, Matt Jones, build a successful golf cart manufacturing business. When the company was sold a year ago, it left Matt with 2.4 million and William with a resume with twenty-five years of experience building three models of golf cart. He now found himself in the mile-high city in mid-January trying his hand at selling R V s. And finally, today showed some promise. He spent the last hour in the stinging wind with an older couple who were determined to score an off-season bargain. They had chosen a beauty. A thirty-nine-foot Rockwood with enough rebates, he stood a good chance of paying some bills this month.

As he held the door to the showroom for the couple, he could see his manger, Kenny, eyeing him from the "Tower," a glass front office on a single step above the showroom floor. The man, a good ten years younger than he, always seemed to harbor contempt for him behind each greeting. He motioned the universal sign for 'come here' with his index finger.

"Please have a seat here." William led his customers to one of the tables dispersed across the showroom floor." Can I get you something to drink?"

"A coffee would be nice." The woman said as she removed her coat. "He'll have one too." The husband dutifully nodded.

William trekked to the tower. Kenny sat with Martinez at the foot of the desk. They both peered up at him with identical slick hair.

"Those folks are Martinez's up," Kenny stated.

"I just spent an hour out on the lot with them," William defended.

"Internet lead," Martinez spat.

"Oh really? What's their names?"

Kenny lifted his hands in the air. "We don't need any clowning around. We are way off quota."

"I've got this," William began.

"No clowns," Kenny halted, "It's Martinez's lead."

William retreated to the break room, his frame shaking with frustration. He poured himself a cup of water, trying to put reason to what he just heard. He took long swigs from the cup, ran his hand through his thinning hair, then nodded to himself.

Kenny was right. Not only was he not a salesman, he was literally a clown. A painted face, goofy outfit Clown. It was the one thing that he wasn't a complete screw up at. He wasn't a good clown by any means. He wasn't that funny. Didn't have an act. But when he put on that costume at the Children's ward in the hospital, the kids lit up. They wanted to see him. Be with him. Bilbo the Clown. For that couple of hours, a week, he felt good. Like he was helping them. Even though he could make no real difference. But then, maybe he never did make a difference in anything. He, for damn sure, wasn't making a difference as a salesman. He crumpled the cup tossed it in the trash and left the building.

Martinez had refreshed the coffees and was presenting a bloated offer to the couple when he noticed their attention was on something behind him. He turned and was surprised to find a clown in the showroom standing just inside the doorway. He returned to the offer. "This should put your payments at about six fifty..."

"You don't see clowns in advertising much anymore," Mrs. Smith said to her husband.

The clown stood motionless, staring across the showroom floor at the group.

"He's not ours," Martinez added as he returned to his task. He couldn't help but look again and was startled to find the clown standing twice as close to them. "Is there something that I can help you with?"

The clown stared motionless, his white gloved hands folded in front of him. He wore a billowy white with red stripe suit with large fuzzy orange buttons down its front. The buttons matched the orange hair that formed a semicircle around the lower back half of a white skull cap. It had a single Cupie doll sprout at the top. His blue painted smile sat motionless and soundless.

Martinez turned his attention back to the couple. "Must be someone's birthday," he offered.

"Oh my!" Mrs. Smith gasped.

Martinez let out a fearful squeak as he found the two-foot-long bulbous red shoes at the back of his chair. "Are you here for a b-birthday?"

The big blue smile just smiled down at him. "Are you a singing telegram?" Martinez offered, "Or something?"

The white grease paint face only smiled down at them. His eyes were directed to the paperwork on the table.

"Can I get someone for you?"

The Clown withdrew a bicycle type horn from the side of his suit. He pointed it at Martinez and squeezed the bellows, emitting a loud honk.

"No no," he said, eyeing the paper work, "Bilbo doesn't think that's going to work."

"What the hell?" Martinez bristled.

"That's much too much." This got a smile from Mrs. Smith.

Bilbo reached into a slit in the other side of his suit and withdrew an extremely large pen, almost two feet in length. He held it up an inch away from his red dot of a nose and stared at it cross eyed. It was the kind that had four different colors to choose from. He licked his lips and selected the red color with an exaggerated push from his index finger.

The commotion drew Kenny's attention from his nest in the tower.

Bilbo scrawled a figure across the paper with his tongue sticking out of the corner of his mouth in concentration. "There," he said, proud of his work, "How's that look?"

The Smiths grinned and nodded in agreement.

"Are you crazy? I can't do that!" Martinez protested.

The horn honked in his face. "Yes you can…"

"No."

Honk! Came the answer.

"No!"

Honk!

"What's going on here?" Kenny asked with a stern look.

Bilbo did an exaggerated jump. "Oh good. This is the manger. He'll make sure that…" He holds his gloved hand to the side of his mouth to block Martinez's view. "This guy doesn't rip you off."

The Smiths smiled from ear to ear, thoroughly enjoying the show.

Kenny sees the paperwork. "I'm sorry but this person doesn't represent this company. We just couldn't do this."

HONK!

Kenny turned angrily and stared through the makeup. Recognition crossed his face. "Bozwick?"

Bilbo carried the remnants of William Bozwick's professional life in a cardboard box to his 2000 Ford Taurus. He brushed the skiff of snow off of its faded green exterior, pausing to look at the foolish clown reflected in the side window.

Bilbo's mood brightened as the warm air of the hospital lobby hit his face as he passed through the door. He stopped in the gift shop and spent his lunch money on five helium balloons. He boarded the elevator and pushed the fifth floor. When the doors slid open, he was the happiest damn clown there ever was.

The station nurse smiled and waved. "Bilbo. What a surprise."

He bowed before her. Happy it wasn't the grouchy nurse Hill.

"The kids are restless today," She added.

He saluted her and turned on his big red heel and marched down the hall.

The first room door was open. Jimmy, a red headed boy of about eight, played with his visiting younger sister without much regard for his open back gown.

"Bilbo!" they sang in unison when they noticed him.

He stood and rubbed his chin, studying the two children. "Well, who do we have here?"

"It's me. Jimmy!" he said as his mother grabbed at his gown, pulling it closed behind him.

"Jimmy huh, and who is this?" He leaned forward to examine the young girl.

"I'm Jennifer," she reported.

"Well, I have a blue balloon for you Jimmy." He extended it to Jennifer.

"No," Jennifer corrected, "I'm Jennifer!"

He snatched it back. "What?" He looks back and forth between the two children. "I see, you are in the wrong places. "Now you stand over here, and you, here." He manipulated them into new positions, and then turned his attention to the balloons. He selected the blue balloon and handed it Jennifer. "Here you go Jimmy."

"No!" sang their response.

Bilbo scratched his head. "You guys keep moving." He hands them two balloons. "Here, you figure it out."

This got a chuckle from their mother and father, who sat watching the show.

"He seems to be feeling better," Bilbo stated

"He should come home tomorrow," She beamed.

"Well, if it isn't my favorite clown."

Bilbo turned at the soft pat on his shoulder. He was pleased to see Dr. Marnau. The one doctor that truly had a heart of gold. The man always greeted everyone with warm affection—patient, staff, or visitor.

"Thanks for coming by again." His warm brown eyes searched his from under bushy white eyebrows. "But you are a hard act to follow." He turned his gaze to his young patient. "It looks like young Jimmy is feeling much better today." He ruffled Jimmy's hair.

"Hey Doc," Bilbo said, getting his attention back. He then lifts his arm to shoulder height. "It hurts when I do this."

Without missing a beat, the Doc answers, "Then don't do that."

Bilbo did a floppy toed soft shoe step, and then threw his arm out in 'ta-da' pose. "See you later kids."

He made his way down the hall, trailing the remaining balloons, happy he hadn't sucked for the kids. He approached the next room, hoping he would not find sweet little Beth. The door was open and there was a small form deeply tucked into the fold of a pillow, watching SpongeBob on TV.

It was Beth, a dark haired five-year-old. His heart sank for her, but he was so happy to see her. He would move heaven and earth if he could somehow make her well. But it was another frustration he had no power over. He eased in the room to see if she was sleeping. Her bright eyes peered up at him from dark circles on a pale little face.

"Bilbo!" she smiled up at him and held out her arms for a hug. He obliged; then tied the balloons to the rail of her bed.

"These things have been following me all day," he said, as he finished the knot. "Would you mind if they stayed with you for a while?"

Her smile grew wider.

"You might need to feed them."

Beth's eyes widened with surprise.

"Watch that green one. It bites."

"Balloons can bite?" she puzzled.

"Just the green ones." His heart warmed with her smile of realization that he was kidding. "Are you feeling better today?"

She shrugged. "I guess so."

"Did your mom come see you today?"

"She's going to come tomorrow," She hoped aloud.

"I know she can't wait to be here." It puzzled him how this little angel had been here for three weeks but he had only seen the girl's mother once, and from what he could gather, she had never known her father. Aside from doctors and nurses, she had no other visitors.

He sat in an awkward silence trying to think of something cheerful to say. "Can I get you anything?" Not his best clown line.

She shook her head, "No," and sank back into her pillow. SpongeBob drawing her weary gaze. He leaned forward and patted her arm with his white gloved hand. She grabbed hold and clung to it.

"I love you," She stated.

That lump in his throat grew unbearably large in an instant. He blinked hard and fast, choking back tears; it would not do to have a blubbering clown. He was completely humbled. He did not deserve such an honor even if it was directed at the symbol of a clown. He could think of no reply. He simply sat, offering his hand which she was content to hold.

His arm grew tired after a while, threatening to cramp, but her grasp remained. He didn't care. He would offer it as long as needed. Soon, her weariness tugged at her eyelids and her grip faded. Her eyes closed as she drifted off. He gently pulled his hand away.

"No," she called out and grasped at his hand, "Don't go."

"I should let you get some sleep," he said.

"No. I'm scared." Her grip grew stronger.

He patted her arm. "What are you scared of?"

"If I go to sleep, it will come."

"What will come?"

"It will come and I won't wake up." She started to sob.

"Nothing's going to hurt you," he assured.

"It wants to take me away. To where I won't wake up." She sobbed with true terror in her pleading eyes.

"What's going to come?" he asked.

"Don't go. Please don't go!" Her voice grew shrill with fear.

He gently brushed her hair back from her face, allowing her to settle back into the pillow.

I'm not going anywhere. It's just some scary dreams. When you're sick, you sometimes have weird dreams."

She reclaimed her grasp on his hand.

"You know that everyone here is doing everything they can to make you better," he assured, "Do you think any of these nice doctors and nurses would let anything come in here to hurt you?"

She considered it, under his smiling gaze, and then shook her head, "No."

"No they sure wouldn't." He grinned. "And I'm going to stay right here so you can sleep, okay?"

She smiled and nodded.

He sat back in one of two chairs in the room. She looked much happier, sleep already tugging at her eyes. Soon her head nodded. She pulled herself from sleep to check that he was still there.

He smiled; then realized that he, too, was weary. He hadn't eaten all day. His thoughts fell back on his own troubles then decided it was a world he didn't wish to visit. He leaned back and rested his own eyes.

He woke with a kink in his neck and tried to put reason to his surroundings. The realization slowly came back to him. He was still in the hospital room, now in the dark. A band of light came in from the hall, falling on the privacy curtain that had somehow been pulled around Beth's bed. He sat and tried to push the fog from his brain.

A shadow appeared on the floor. It crept toward the bed. He leaned forward to see what caused it. There was no one there. Was he still asleep? He blinked and looked at the floor again. The shadow grew until it fell upon the curtain. He rose to his feet and looked again for the source of the shadow. Nothing. He sprang forward and tore back the curtain. He was surprised to see a figure crouched over Beth's small form.

"Bilbo." Dr. Marnau smiled up at him, and then pulled the child's blankets up to her chin. He stepped away and whispered to him, "I hope I didn't wake you." "No. I should have left a long time ago," he said, "She's just been so scared."

The doctor put his hand on his shoulder. "As far as I'm concerned, visiting hours don't exist if it benefits a patient."

Bilbo studied Beth's shallow breathing. "Why is she so scared?"

"She's fighting for her life," he offered, "The poor thing. And I'll be damned if I can't help her." He joined Bilbo's gaze. "It's a hell of a thing, the suffering of the innocent."

"What can we do?"

"Keep up hope," he offered, "I have specialist coming in. And I'll keep bringing them no matter what it takes. Something is causing this. To know what that is would be the key." He looked into Bilbo's eyes. "But you keep bringing the fun and joy."

"I don't know if I even do that."

"Sure you do." He patted his back again. "Well I should be about my rounds. You stay as long as you like."

Bilbo stood alone looking down at the girl. The dark circles under her eyes seemed more pronounced. Her face seemed thinner; her cheek bones, more visible than they did before his nightmare laden sleep. "God, how could you do this to such an innocent?" He sat back down and stared down at his long red shoes, realizing he was still a clown. A silly clown in a serious world. About as useful a rubber chicken to a surgeon. What was he going to do with his wreck of a life.

He almost didn't hear it. A gentle squeak of orthopedic shoes at the door way. He looked up to see the small frame of a Nun standing with and old-fashioned carpet bag at her side. She shuffled in and sat down next to him with a "humph" of relief and settled her old bones into the chair. She looked at Beth's sleeping form. "How is she?"

"Resting" was all that he could think to say.

The Nun bent over and opened the bag. She withdrew knitting needles and the beginnings of a project. "You must be Bilbo."

"Ah yes." He answered with surprise.

"I'm Martha, Martha Sledge." She stated as the needles began their soft rhythmic clicking.

His eye widened with further surprise. "You're Sister Sledge?"

"Oh have you heard of me?"

"Sort'a," he laughed, "You're a bit paler than I imagined."

"Oh I don't get out in the sunshine too much." She answered, matter of factly, "Black is so hot in the sun."

"That makes sense," he nodded in agreement.

The old woman looked at Beth, concern on her face. She then turned her gaze to him and smiled. "She is fortunate to have a protector like you."

He laughed bitterly. "Fortunate. God is letting her suffer needlessly, probably to death. And as for me, I'm not a protector. I can't do anything. I can't even hold down a job." He grabbed his costume as if to pull it to her. "Look at me. This is the real me. I'm a damn Clown."

She leaned over and patted his knee. "Even superheroes have special suits," she assured, then resumed her needle work.

He shook his head and leaned back in his chair. "I wish I could do something," he mumbled, and then sat forward in his chair. "I should get something to eat," he said, mostly to himself.

"You know that God uses the foolish things to shame the intelligent," the Nun stated, never looking up from her knitting.

Bilbo rolled his eyes her direction. "Huh?"

"And the weak to confound the strong?"

He slapped his knees with his hands "Oakey doakey," he said, as he rose to his feet. "It was nice meeting you."

"Oh, I have something you might like." She said, as she rummaged in her bag. "Something I don't think anyone else would appreciate." She withdrew an oversized pair of novelty sunglasses. The kind that were twice as wide as the wearer's head. "Here." She presented them in all their cheap red plastic glory.

"Hey, where did you find these?" he asked, truly interested.

"I have my sources."

He took them and put them on and glanced around the room. "These are great."

"Good, you enjoy them," she said, "Maybe they will help you see things clearly."

"Wow, thanks," he said gratefully.

"Pretty soon you won't even need them."

"Huh?" he puzzled.

"Never mind. You go get something to eat. I'm going to sit here with Beth a while."

"Thanks again," he said, and he left the room.

Bilbo walked out with thoughts of the cafeteria, and his new sunglasses on, dwarfing his face.

He skidded to a stop and jumped back a step in fear. In front of him slithered a large snake. It was the most massive serpent he had ever seen. Its girth was over a foot across. Its even wider head slithered away from him a good twenty feet down the vacant hallway. Its color was a bizarre red color, like blood, itself. It faded into a deep purple at each tip of a forked tail at his feet. He pulled off the glasses for a better look. The creature began to fade away, leaving only bare tile. He put the glasses back on. There it was, continuing its trek into the next wing. He followed, mesmerized by the bizarre sight. Then other movement drew his attention to the walls and ceiling. Strange black creatures skittered across the surfaces before him. They appeared to be some kind of a hybrid of a spider and a crab. Their movement too fast to get a good look at. The huge serpent methodically made its way across the hospital wing, its tongue sampling the air. It continued straight at the wall, and then disappeared through the wall an inch at a time as if it broke the surface of a lake. He stood and stared at the spot for a few moments, and then bent down and probed the surface of the wall with his fingers. It was solid. He scratched his head and turned to leave. As he turned, he glimpsed a figure standing at a patient's bed through the open door of a nearby room. It was human shaped in form, but there the similarity ended. It was tall and slender. Its flesh was pale, almost opaque. The red and blue blood veins that coursed through its body were the only real color the thing possessed. Its grotesque back was to him as it hunched over the bed of an overweight, middle aged patient, who moaned in pain. He cautiously entered the room both fascinated and repulsed by the grotesque form. Its back narrowed to a buttocks of sorts. It had the shape of a buttocks but lacked the defining crack that most humans possessed. Below, that came to almost shapeless legs that ended in veiny clumps of meat for feet.

Neither it nor the man in the bed paid him any mind as he moved around it for a closer look. He let out a frightened gasp when he saw its face. Its head had no hair— just pulsing veins under the skin. Its ears were merely holes with a tiny flap of skin above each one. Its face was almost featureless with a tiny slit for a mouth. But it was the eyes that made him shudder. Or, was it the lack of eyes? They were just two black holes. Like the Black holes in space that he learned of as a kid. Dark collapsed suns that sucked in all matter with crushing force. They seemed to be drawing its own flesh into its two bottomless recesses.

Its long lanky arms reached down to the man's belly where they seemed to grow right into it. Its arms wrenched back and forth as if it were wringing out a wet dish towel inside the man's abdomen. With each twist, the man moaned. The morphine drip that poured through his IV, almost useless.

Bilbo considered his options for a moment as he studied the thing. He sheepishly extended his hand in front of it. It had no interest in anything but its morbid work. Bilbo boldly waved his hand in its face. Still no reaction. It either didn't see him or just didn't care about his presence. He looked down at the man who was pale and pouring sweat.

Bilbo sucked in a large breath, and then readied himself to touch the thing. He paused, and then went for it. His white gloved hands grasped the cold clammy flesh. He could feel its muscles flex in his grip as they worked. He pulled, and then pushed it but couldn't move it. Its gaze remained unchanged, focused on its task. He put his back into it, grunting with effort. He might as well have been trying to move a ten-ton statue. He backed away and took off the glasses. He studied it until it faded away, leaving only the suffering patient. Bilbo stepped back. It was all too much for him. The glasses slid into the oversized pocket of his suit as he walked away.

William woke to the ringing phone. He pulled himself up and stared blankly until his brain caught up what his senses told him. He still had bits of grease paint on the side of his face that he was too tired to notice. He fumbled under his clown suit at the foot of his bed. He found the phone and pushed answer.

"Yes, hello."

"Hi William," the voice began, "My name is Seth Baxter. I'm sorry to call on such short notice; Dr. Murnau gave me your name. He said you do work as a clown."

He sat dumbfounded.

"I have a toy store in the Southwest Plaza Mall and I'm having a grand opening today. I have found myself short one clown. Would you be interested?"

He nodded then answered. "Yes. Yes, I'll be there."

He was in costume within an hour. He found his keys next to the oversized glasses. He picked up the glasses and thought about putting them on. He decided against it and shoved them into the long deep pockets of his costume.

He felt good. It was good to be working. He didn't even know how much he was being paid but the work was easy. He stood at the entrance of the bustling noisy store and handed out coupons. He even did a little shtick for those who would pause for it. Even the endless mechanical barking and flipping of the toy dog in its table top pen wasn't getting to him. Although he might buy one so he could smash it after his shift. He worked between the mechanical mutt and a display of old school red rubber balls sat at either side of the entrance to the store. The real stuff of interest resided inside. He was considering finding something to drink when he heard it. Pop, pop, pop. It sounded like fire crackers at the far end of the mall. Then came screams. He looked up to see an onrush of people running toward him, down the hub of the mall. They dropped or tossed aside their cumbersome shopping bags and darted into shop entrances where they could. It was the splintering impacts to the smart phone kiosk to his left that made him realize he was hearing gun shots.

He surveyed down the aisle and saw a woman frantically pushing a stroller, spilling a sippy cup onto the floor. She just made the intersection at which he stood and ducked around the corner as a bullet whizzed by.

"Thank you Lord" was all he could say. Then he saw another woman. She darted from the edge of a storefront into the center of the Isle. Her considerable girth made her slow and an easy target. Two more pops sent her sprawling face first onto the gleaming mall floor not twenty feet in front of him.

He stood stunned, staring down the hallway. A lone figure strode down the center of the walkway. He wore a long black trench coat from which he pulled a fresh magazine. He released the spent magazine on the Glock with his thumb and let it drop to the floor and inserted the new one without diverting his gaze. The gunman's gaze locked onto Bilbo.

"Put on the glasses."

Did he hear it? Did he think it? Bilbo wasn't sure. But he did it.

The gunman now was covered with some kind of creatures. They were about the size of small monkeys. There was one clinging to each one of his limbs, there was one at his torso and one clung to the back of his neck. Bilbo was shocked at their appearance. They appeared the classic devil form. Their leathery skin, a dark cherry red. Spade tipped tails wrapped around the man's limbs aiding their hold. Their hands burrowed through the man's clothes and into his very flesh where the seemed to control the man's movement by manipulating his very muscles and tendons like the man was a flesh covered puppet. Their faces were human like but topped with two small horns above the foreheads. Their eyes were oily black beads. And all of those eyes were locked on him.

Bilbo grabbed three of the red balls from the display. He started juggling them. He carefully started walking toward the gunman, praying his feeble juggling skill would not fail him as he proceeded. The two men approached each other. The gun man's barrel lowered a bit.

Bilbo could see the man's face clearly now as he was only feet away. He was surprised to see the boyish feature of an acne covered face. His chubby cheeks were only months from childhood. The other face that peered over his right shoulder was far more sinister. It seemed to smirk as its arms ran up under the base of the man's skull through his neck. Its black eyes were locked on him and his performance. At about four feet from the man, Bilbo stopped. He caught two of the balls with his left hand and one in the right. He extended the ball palm up toward the man. All the faces studied the ball, and then looked at him bewildered.

The man cocked his head slightly. "This doesn't make sense," he puzzled. In a flash, the man shoved the Glock's barrel under his own chin.

"No!" Bilbo tried for the gun. But action beats reaction. And the reaction was suddenly in slow motion. He saw the pad of the man's finger blush as it pressed the trigger just out of his reach. Then the deafening blast as the bullet passed through the man's brain turning his head into a grotesque party popper of blood, gray matter, and bone. He even heard the bullet impact the steel rafters of the ceiling. As the body crumpled to the floor, the demons leaped from it. Then a chorus of high-pitched laughter filled the air as the creatures grabbed their round bellies so amused with what they had caused. One fell to the tile and pounded its fist, overcome with laughter. They then scurried away back down the aisle way, one hurtling over the body of the women. Bilbo watched until they disappeared around a distant intersection. He then reexamined the carnage and finally the red balls in his hand. One thing was for sure, "This doesn't make sense."

It was night before he finished with the police. He told them all he felt they would believe. He wasn't that sure what he believed. All that he could focus on were the tiny splatters of blood on the glasses he held in his hands and tried to process the questions.

Anxiety churned at his core as he pushed out the door into the brisk night air. It had been a while, but right now he needed a beer. He needed to calm his nerves. He found an out-of-the-way bar called *Schooners*. It was close and to hell with changing. He went in full clown apparel.

It was one of those dark places with a few tables and a bar at the back of the room. Behind the length of a bar ran a mirror lined with glass shelves of liquor bottles, to give the place the allusion of being bigger than it was. As he entered, he drew chuckles from a couple seated near the door. The only other people in the place were a man doting over his drink at the bar and the bartender, transfixed by his Smartphone. He took at seat at the bar.

"So a clown walks into a bar..." the bartender said, glancing over his phone.

This invoked a hearty laugh from the man at the end stool.

"There's got to be punch line here somewhere," he jested.

"Yeah, yeah. Could I get a beer?" Bilbo answered.

"Anything in particular?" he asked

"Whatever's on tap," he answered, "Please."

"One draw for the clown. Coming right up."

Bilbo studied his reflection between the bottles in the mirror across the bar as he waited. There was something just above the upturned corner of his big blue smile. A dark speck. Like a mole. A mole that he never applied. His gloved finger removed it. He examined the dark crusted speck on the white fabric of his index finger.

Dried blood.

Nausea churned within him and he felt himself flush. If his face wasn't already painted white, he knew that he would be.

"Here you go." The bartender placed the foamy beverage before him.

"Ah, thanks," he answered. But all that he could think of was the lives that were snuffed out before him. People who woke up this morning the same as him, just trying to improve their situations. And now...

Tink. Tink. He heard something. A soft tapping sound, like a fingernail tapping on a glass bottle. Then the man's drink order at the end of the bar drowned it out. Then, 'tink'. He heard it again. His gaze was drawn to the bottles at the mirror before him. Then to one bottle in particular. A bottle of tequila. There writhing in the amber liquid was the pale grub, very much alive. It wriggled violently as if in hot ashes, occasionally ramming its nub of a head into the glass with a soft tink.

Bilbo glanced around. No one else paid any attention. He reached into his side pocket and withdrew the glasses. He carefully opened them up and placed them on his face.

The display of bottles suddenly came alive with motion. Most of the bottles teemed with black eel-like creatures that franticly searched a way out of their glass prisons. Others were spinney slug like things clung to the side of the glass. His own drink boiled with sleek black activity. He carefully grasped the bottom of the glass with both hands and pushed it away.

"Where can I get a pair of those?"

The voice startled him. He looked to the man at the end of the bar. "What?"

"Those glasses," he answered and punctuated it with a stifled belch.

Bilbo looked at the man and became transfixed with his face, something moved just under the skin of his cheek. Another thing moved across the man's forehead—the size and shape of the things that he was witnessing.

"I don't think that you would like them." Bilbo replied.

"Who wouldn't like a snazzy pair like that?"

Bilbo only shrugged as he watched the man bring his drink to his lips. More of the eel things slithered between his lips and into his mouth.

He placed the mostly empty glass on the bar and called to the bartender. "Better set'em up again."

"Well," Bilbo slapped his knees and stood, "That's enough for one day." He pulled some crumpled bills from his pocket and placed them on the bar. "Thank you, gentlemen. It's time to call it a night."

It was two days since the incident and William had not left the house. The world was just too scary, and that was before those damn glasses. Was it real? Or, was his wreck of a life finally cracking him up? He wasn't sure, but he couldn't bring himself to put them on again.

After staring into an almost empty refrigerator, he searched the *Help Wanted* ads and saw all the opportunities for those people who had skills and talents. He tossed the paper aside. His thoughts kept turning to Beth and the hospital. He thought of her lying there scared and alone.

He got up and headed for his garage. He pushed through the door and stepped down the two steps where he looked over the two cluttered stalls.

He could see his breath.

He looked at the 72 Chevy Nova that took up one stall, mostly in pieces. Its front clip was propped in various places along the walls as the chassis sat pushed against the back wall. The engine that sat on an engine stand just in front of it. It was the only part of turning his high school car into a mean street machine that he had managed to complete. He had poured five thousand dollars into it alone. But that was when he was gainfully employed and the pursuit of such things seemed possible. Now maybe he could sell it. The next stall housed another project that no longer seemed prudent. It was a home built "Clown Car." He had fashioned it on an extended and beefed up golf cart frame. He fashioned the body to loosely resemble a topless model-A. Although exaggerated. It was painted white with multi colored polka-dots on it. It had a large key shape extending from the trunk meant to resemble a windup toy. It was mostly complete but needed some kind of power plant. But he doubted that it would see a parade anytime soon. He went to a cabinet and pulled out a quart of oil. The Taurus would be needing it. He glanced out the garage window. It was already getting dark.

The Taurus pulled into the icy hospital parking lot and found a space. Its door screeched open and two large red clown shoes dropped to the pavement, and then were filled with Bilbo's stocking feet. He glanced back at the big pair of glasses that sat on the passenger seat. He decided not to bring them. He climbed out and gazed up at the multi story building. A shiver overcame him. He wasn't sure it was the cold night air that caused it.

The elevator doors opened and Bilbo stepped out and strode down the hallway. Out of the corner of his eye, he thought he saw it as he passed the first room on his right— the hideous Gumby thing that he had encountered on his last visit. But as he stopped and looked in, it wasn't there. He stepped to the door and recognized the patient. It was the same man, and no better off.

He made his way to Beth's room. The door stood open so he eased in. There was no one there. Only a neatly made bed. He turned and made his way back to the Nurses station, glancing into every room he passed as he did.

There was still no one at the station as he searched behind the counter.

"Hello!" he called, as he frantically patted the counter top, "Anyone here?" He glanced around. "Hello!"

"Yes" came a voice from behind him.

He turned to see a nurse exiting the room behind him.

"Sorry," he apologized, "Could you tell me where Beth, the young girl at the end, is?"

"Oh, she's been moved."

"Moved? Moved were?"

"I'm sorry," she soothed, "She's been moved to intensive care."

"Intensive care!" Bilbo took off toward the elevator.

"You'll have to be family to see her!" she called after him.

The elevator doors couldn't open fast enough. His big shoes slapped the floor as he briskly strode down the hall. The ward opened into a round room with the Nurses station in the middle. The station had a counter that surrounded the nurses work area, allowing them to see all the rooms that literally surrounded them. The dark haired nurse, Hill, looked up from her work and held her hand up, indicating halt.

"No. No, not this ward!" she warned.

Bilbo's eyes searched the rooms that have mostly glass fronts, for easy viewing, with about three foot finely finished wood skirting at the floor and at the ceiling that gave it a richer, more elegant look. He didn't see her but two of the rooms had the privacy curtain pulled around the beds.

"Which room is Beth...."

"This is the Intensive Care Ward," she drilled, "There are no visitors allowed."

"I just need to know how she is," he pleaded.

"Unless you are immediate family, you're going to have to leave."

"Just tell me how she is."

"You'll have to ask at the main desk," she informed, shooshing him away.

"Listen, I just want a little information," he said, as calmly as he could.

"You have to leave."

Bilbo saw red. "You don't have to be a bitch..."

"Out!" she ordered, "Now!"

"Hey, hey." Dr. Marnau's hand grasped his arm. "Bilbo. Calm down."

He turned to face the doctor. "Sorry Doctor, I'm just trying to get some information on Beth."

"Of course," he consoled. "She's taken a turn for the worse, I'm afraid," he firmly grasped his shoulder, "She has slipped into coma."

"What's wrong?" Bilbo pleaded, "What's causing this?"

"We are running some tests. We should know more by morning. In the meantime, we have her here under constant watch."

Bilbo's head dropped in dejection.

"Maybe we can take a quick peek."

The nurse glared at him. "Doctor, you know the regulations. Only immediate family."

Doctor Marnau gave an irritated nod and turned back to Bilbo. "Come back tomorrow, I'll be able to tell you more." He gazed into his eyes. "Okay?"

Bilbo nodded.

Bilbo was seething as he marched back to the elevator. Something was not right about this whole thing. He had to get a look with the glasses. A look at Nurse Hill. Was something controlling her? Was something latched onto Beth?

The creepy crawly spiders with claws skittered before him as he marched back through the hall with the glasses on. He came upon the grotesque creature still at its cruel work on that poor man. Rage surged through Bilbo's frame. He broke into a sprint and rammed shoulder first into the back of the thing. The air was forced from his lungs and sharp pain shot from his shoulder as he collapsed to the floor. The creature stood unfazed, never diverting its attention from its work. That just pissed Bilbo off. He climbed to his feet and began punching it in the kidneys until his fists ached. It was as if he wasn't even there. His rage rose to bursting as he backed off and frantically searched for a weapon. His gaze fell of a fire extinguisher of the wall. He smashed the glass and pulled it free. With all the force he could muster, he drove it into the back of its head. He thrust again and again. It had no effect. It didn't even leave a mark. He grasped the extinguisher handle with both hands, stepped back, and spun around swinging it like an Olympic Hammer thrower. At the end of his fifth revolution, he impacted its head with a loud clang. The room filled with the flame-retardant powder as the trigger broke from the tank. Bilbo tumbled to the floor, engulfed in a white fog.

As the powder cleared, he found that he had finally drawn the attention of the demon. He shivered as its vacant eye holes were turned upon him. Its gaze froze him for a moment; then its head turned back to peer down on the man in whom its hands were imbedded. Bilbo let his head fall back defeated.

"Oh Lord, just make it go away," he moaned.

He lay there a long moment and stared at the ceiling. He then wearily climbed to his feet and was surprised to find only the bed and its patient. He fanned his hand where the thing had been and lifted the glasses off his nose to look under them.

Nope, nothing there. The thing was gone.

The man in the bed began to stir. Bilbo looked around at the powder coated mess and decided that he should probably get out there. Moments later, a nurse entered the room. She stopped short, taking in the room.

"What in the world?" she wondered. She saw her patient stir and rushed to his side. His white caked eyelids fluttered open.

"Are you alright?" she asked.

His eyes searched for a moment. "Yeah," he smiled, "I'm feeling pretty good."

Bilbo made his way to the intensive care ward, brushing the white talc from his costume as he went. He eased down the hall, adjusting the glasses to be sure and see everything. He had to get a look at that nurse. But as he arrived at the station, no one was there.

Not the way an intensive care unit should be run, he thought. He made it to the counter top, rested his arm on it and searched over the edge. Nothing. No nurse, no creepy crawlies, nothing. He glanced around at the rooms. His heart leaped as he recognized Beth's small form in the room directly ahead. He quietly entered, cautiously scanning the room. She looked so small and so vulnerable. A tiny form neatly tucked into the large hospital bed. He searched the floor then under the bed. He searched every corner of the room. Nothing demonic. He turned his attention back to Beth. He leaned over, examined her. He adjusted his glasses as the examined her arm. No strange creatures—only the black intravenous tubes running from her arm.

He grasped the tubing in his fingertips. Since when was surgical tubing black? This looked more like fuel line in a car. He traced to a stand at the side of the bed. The lines ran into an antique looking wooden box with glass sides. Not the equipment he expected to see in this state-of-the-art medical facility. Inside were small leathery bellows that pumped over a small glass bottle that was filled with... well, with light. Bright blue light.

Dr. Marnau stood and watched Bilbo study the device. "You can see," he said aloud. Bilbo was startled and whipped around at the sound of the voice. He found no one behind him. No one in the room.

"How long have you been able to see?" the doctor asked.

Bilbo's gaze was drawn upward towards the ceiling. There on the wooden header, just above the glass wall, stood the good Doctor. Bilbo tried to put reason to what he was seeing. Defying the laws of reason not to mention gravity. The doctor stood on the wall with his arms folded and causally leaned back into the ceiling.

Before he could form another thought, the doctor's face melted from his human mask into gray angular demonic features and his eyes turned an unholy oily black. It screeched, showing fang-like teeth and pounced down on him, driving its fist into his head with brutal force. Bilbo collapsed to the floor, knocked out cold as the glasses slid to the corner of the room.

Bilbo slowly came around. Objects came back into focus as he tried to put sense to them. He saw the doctor thing hunch over the bed; it had Beth's tiny heel in its mouth. Its throat worked as it swallowed the girl's life blood. It suddenly let the limb drop to the bed. It glanced at Bilbo as it licked blood from its thin gray lips. Bilbo played dead. It turned its attention to the box at the side of the bed. Its small bellows has stopped pumping. Inside the tiny bottle glowed brilliant blue light. Only, it was liquid. Like a liquid welding arc of brilliance.

Its long slender talon-like nails forced open the box. It lifted out the bottle, pulled the tubing from it, and snapped close a silver lid. It then gazed into the light with satisfaction.

Bilbo quietly climbed to his feet behind it. He charged it, impacting its back with his shoulder and drove it into the glass of the outside window. He grabbed it under its crotch and lifted as the glass gave way into a shower of razor-sharp shards. He pushed with all of his might and sent it out the sixth story as he stumbled to the floor with the glass. He climbed back to his feet shaking off glass and looked out through the newly formed opening. He could see the glint from the street lights reflecting off the shards of glass of the grass below but no crumpled body was to be seen. The small glowing vile sat precariously on the window sill. He carefully picked it up and gazed into its brilliance. This was important.

The gray hand shot through the opening with the speed of a cobra, and clasped around Bilbo's hand and the vile. Bilbo tried to grasp the bottle as the creature's other hand came to pry open his grip. Impossibly strong, it forced open his grip and retrieved the vile. The creature's black eyes leered down on him from the top of the window frame. It looked at the vile now in its own hand, smiled, and then looked back at Bilbo. It shook its raised index finger from side to side.

"What the hell is going on here?" the nurse's voice cried from outside the room.

The creature rose to its feet on the outside wall and strode down its vertical surface as easily as it would across a football field.

Bilbo turned back to Beth with concern.

"What are you doing?" the nurse fumed as she entered the room.

"Is she alright?" Bilbo asked, as he looked for signs of life.

The nurse looked at the carnage. "Did you break the window?"

"Is she alright?" Bilbo pleaded, "Is she alive?"

She quickly slipped on her stethoscope and placed the probe on her chest. "She's breathing." She tenderly grasped her wrist. "Her pulse is weak"

Bilbo took off in a sprint. His big red shoes slapping the floor.

"Don't you go anywhere," the nurse called, "Stop!"

He made it out the front entrance in time to see a black BMW pull out from the physician's only parking. He could see that its interior and the doctor's face was illuminated the shade of blue. His chest heaving, he again broke into a run for the parking lot and his car. The street lights reflected off the ice glazed pavement as he struggled in the slick clown shoes. As a shadow crossed over him, he felt the sudden displacement of air above him. He crouched and slid to his left. Something grabbed at him as it passed over. He looked up to see large leathery wings pumping a man-sized creature back up into the darkness beyond the street lights.

The Taurus sat about seventy yards away. His feet kept slipping as he tried to gain purchase on the slick asphalt. It would soon be circling back. The smooth leather of the soles of his shoes slid and spun out as he moved as fast as he could. An otherworldly shriek came from above but the creature was lost beyond the bright street lights. Half the distance had been closed when the ten-foot wingspan broke through the light. Its human like face smiled as its talon fingered arms stretched out before it. Bilbo dove to the ground just out of reach of it snapping grasp. It landed and slid on the icy surface and used its razor sharp black clawed feet and one hand to dig into the asphalt, never taking its gaze off its prey. Bilbo sprang to his feet, his legs churning towards his car as the demon stood erect. It studied him a moment, its spade tail twitching behind it— then strode after him.

Bilbo slid into his car door and grasped the handle. He shuffled backward and thank God, the door screeched open in his grasp. The demon stepped up behind him folding back its bat like wings. Its muscular frame stood a good two feet taller than him. Bilbo threw himself into the car and pulled the door closed.

The demon bent down and peered in at the terrified clown's face staring back. Bilbo's white gloved finger sheepishly reached up and depressed the lock button. The demon let out an ear-splitting screech, spraying sputum at the window. Bilbo answered with his own high-pitched scream as a little pee escaped into his pants. The demon raised its clenched fists into the air and brought them crashing down onto the roof of the car. The force of the blow caved in the roof and shattered most of the car's glass.

Bilbo crouched as low as he could as the roof panel collapsed closer and closer to him as it impacted it again and again. The demon's hand gripped the top of the drivers' door and ripped it from its hinges, and then sent it sailing across the parking lot.

Bilbo made himself as small as he could, readying himself to die.

The rumble of a car engine grew as headlights swept across his face as he looked up. The thing had disappeared as a slick black '57 Chevrolet pulled up next to him. Even as terrified as he was, he couldn't help but admire the car's perfect finish and the healthy rumble of its engine. He pulled himself from the twisted, metal searching for the demon. It was nowhere to be seen. He then tried to see into the car's darkly tinted passenger window. The door popped open. He reached down and pulled it open. There sat the small and frail Sister Sledge behind the large steering wheel.

"Looks like you could use a lift," she stated, as she pulled her bag to her from the passenger side of the seat.

"Ah yeah, I guess I would." He slid in next to her. "Nice car."

"Yes, it's my father's," she said, as she backed out of the parking slot. She put the car in gear and roared out of the parking lot. She then reached into her bag and pulled out the novelty glasses. "Nurse Hill said she found these on the floor." She handed it to him.

Bilbo took them. They must have fallen off when he got hit. He had seen everything without them.

"She said you went a little crazy." "She may be right," he answered, "But she didn't see the whole thing."

Sister Sledge nodded as she accelerated through a yellow light.

"These glasses," Bilbo said, as he looked down at them; "The things I see, they are real but what am I seeing? Where do they come from?"

The Sister maneuvered the car around slower traffic across the icy surface. "The spiritual world has always existed around us, but our Father has seen fit to shield it from our eyes."

"These things are demons?"

The sister nodded as he manipulated the steering wheel.

"So why give these to me?" he asked, as he gripped the armrest his eyes forced to focus on the road.

The sister shrugged. "I do not understand the ways of the Father. I only seek to do his will."

Bilbo pulled the safety belt across his lap and clasped it. "So, Vampires do exist?"

She glanced over at him with surprise. "You have seen a Vampire?"

"Doctor Marnue." he stated

"No," she answered, searching his face.

"Car," he pointed, as he tensed in his seat.

She maneuvered around more traffic.

"Vampires do exist, but not like you think," she said. "When someone willingly submits to the demon of Vampirism and voluntarily coexists with it, they can gain its supernatural powers. They cannot die as long as they yield their bodies to the immortal demon."

"Oh," he said, like it made complete sense. "And what is the liquid light?"

"Liquid light?" She echoed.

"It seemed to be extracting, well, light from her with some kind of machine," he explained.

"Oh, no." She gasped, and then seemed to fall into deep thought.

Bilbo waited in silence for her to continue. She did not. "Oh no. Oh no what?"

"It seems the good doctor is not satisfied with causing suffering and stealing the life blood of his victims," she answered gravely. "It looks like he's found a way to extract their very souls." She made the sign of the cross and drifted back into deep thought.

Bilbo considered this as the sister fishtailed the car onto the interstate heading into the city. It was too much to handle. Demons, Vampires, stolen souls. It was beyond reason, and here he was, right in the middle of it. What possible effect could he have on the situation? If God was choosing him to do something, it must be a mistake. He squirmed in his seat. He had to get out of here. Go somewhere far away from it. Then he thought of little Beth. What will become of her?

"You know," sister Sledge began, "The Lord equips those he calls. He will never let you suffer more than you can endure."

"Great!" he answered, "I can endure way more than I want to. I'm already enduring way freaking more than I want. It's what I can endure that scares me."

He hoped she was right. He hoped that he could somehow save Beth. He put on the glasses and gazed out the windshield at the city. Its buildings rose under a canopy of clouds that glowed amber from the city lights. In the center of it stood a dark figure towering above the buildings. A gleaming black demon with horns on its head. Its eyes glowed a deep red like the fires of hell. Its long arms stretched out, moving back and forth over the city; its long slender fingers moved up and down as if it were operating unseen marionettes.

Bilbo sat back and closed his eyes. What could he possibly do?

The Chevy rumbled up to the front of his house, its tires crunched to a stop on refrozen slush. The Sister turned to him, her gaze filled with earnest compassion. "Times like this require much prayer and fasting."

Bilbo could only nod at her as he pulled the door handle.

"Don't be too hasty in whatever you do." She said.

He stepped out of the car and closed the door. He waved as the car pulled away. Then he looked up at the massive black demon that towered above the city. It didn't seem to pay him any mind.

William stood in the shower, carefully feeling the lump on his head. It was very tender. His thoughts went back to the day, at the ripe old age of twelve, that he accepted Christ as his savior. He remembered the times that he felt 'His' presence in his life and experienced answered prayer. Shame overcame him as he realized that Jesus had progressively taken a back seat in his life as he pursued the enticements of this world. He had failed that pursuit and failed God. In fact, failure is what he did best.

He took Sister Sledge's advice and began to pray. At first, it was hard to concentrate. All he could do was ask, 'what could I do?' Then outside thought would pull his attention from prayer. But he forced himself to stay on task and somehow find out what the God of the universe could possibly have to say to him.

He found himself in the garage, unsure of how much time had passed. He looked over the projects. This time he felt inspired and set to work. He felt empowered. His mind was sharp and sure. He could see how to make things work. Things went together as he envisioned and without the usual unrelenting difficulty of which he was accustomed.

It may have been hours or it may have been days, he was not sure. All he knew was that he was hungry and very tired. He went into the house and to his room where he collapsed into bed; he fell asleep asking God for guidance.

It was before sunrise and he was fully awake. Grumbles erupted from his gut. He was starving, but he refused to eat until he was sure he was moving in the direction God wanted him to go. He shuffled to his closet and pulled open the door. As he filed through the shirts, the scarred butt stock of his grandfather's shotgun caught his eye at the bottom of the closet. He pulled it from behind the clothing. He smiled as he remembered when his grandfather had given it to him after a lengthy lecture on firearm safety. He was so proud to be able to go hunting with him and his dad. His hand ran down the scuffed and marred stock of the double barreled 12-gauge. He chuckled as he recalled how it almost knocked him on his butt the first few times, he shot it. From the shelf above, he pulled a box of shells; it contained a few # 2 shotshells he had used for goose and a single shell of buckshot. He propped the gun over his shoulder and headed back to the garage.

With the gun in the vice, he paced back and forth with a hacksaw in his hand.

"Grandpa would not approve," he thought aloud, as he tapped the hacksaw against his leg.

"Ah, heck." He set to work cutting the majority of its two barrels off. After some major huffing and puffing and a lengthy break, he started cutting the rear of the butt stock off behind the pistol grip portion. He roughly fashioned the rest of it into a pistol grip with a file. After locating a length of paracord, he made a lanyard that he could hang around his neck and let the weapon hang just below his waist.

That done, he sat the project on the bench and stared down at it. With his fingers drumming the bench top, he glanced around room. He spied a couple of wooden mop handles. He placed them on the bench. He then pulled a plastic tub from under the bench and opened it. It was full of junk. He rifled through it, and then paused. "Hmm." He pulled out two red shock absorber boots and placed them on the bench. After a bit more digging, he withdrew an old pets' squeaky toy. He squeaked it a couple of times then threw it onto the bench. He then went to his toolbox, pulled open the bottom drawer and withdrew a two-pound sledge hammer. He held it up and inspected it.

"That should do." Using the shock absorber boots, the squeaker from the toy, and some bright blue paint, he soon fashioned the hammer into what looked like a child's toy. Complete with a sharp squeak when hammered. "Now there's a hammer a clown would use."

The sun was rising again and William realized he still hadn't eaten. It reminded him to keep praying. He called the hospital, knowing he could not set foot in there again. Beth was still alive but in a coma. That is all he could find out.

He decided that he had to find that little bottle that contained her soul. He would bring it back to her. He would restore her health. And this time, he would make a difference. At least in her world. But where would the doctor take it? His home? If so, how could he find it? He booted up the computer, typed in the doctor's name. A White Pages search brought up his phone number and address. He put the address into a map search. He got a map and directions to a Lookout Mountain location. Could it be that easy? He went to the kitchen and made himself a sandwich.

He had gathered up a backpack full of equipment that he thought he might need, when the thought of a flashlight hit him. He pulled open kitchen draws and pushed its contents around until he came across a long sleek black Mag light. He thumbed the on button. No light. There was a lone D-cell battery in the drawer but who knew if it was even any good. He opened another drawer and began stirring around its contents. His motion stopped as a warm smile crossed his face. He withdrew an object, cradling it in his hand as if it were a tiny baby. It was a shiny metal flashlight that he had gotten as a kid. His father had purchased it for him at his first and only visit to the circus. He smiled at the plastic lion's head that surrounded the bulb. He slid the button forward with his thumb and was surprised to see a strong beam of light that emitted from the lions open mouth.

"Awesome," he said.

The clown suit was cleaned and ironed. He would be at his best. Every detail of the costume was perfect. But as he sat and applied the makeup, he could not bring himself to put on the big blue smile. Not while Beth was in such dire straits. Not while demons ran amuck and causing pain and suffering. The best he could do was a big blue frown.

The garage door rattled open under the power of its electric opener. The headlights of the little clown car ignited into brilliance as it roared to life. The V-8 engine was deafeningly loud as its exhaust exploded directly from its headers that protruded from the engine compartment. The car's stance strained against its brakes as Bilbo put it into gear. He placed the glasses on his face and zipped up a large orange parka over his clown suit. He grabbed the small steering wheel that was directly between his knees in the miniscule cockpit and eased the car into the cold night air. He made his way to the highway and headed west toward the mountains and opened it up. The colossal black demon continued its dark work over the city. Only, this time its gaze tracked the tiny clown car as it sped towards the dark mountains.

Bilbo parked in a pullout on the road he figured was close to the address he had found. He climbed out of the car and slowly straightened as he grabbed the small of his back. He cupped his hands and blew into them trying to bring warmth back to them. He caught sight of a light through the dense thicket of evergreen trees.

"I hope that's it," he told himself, as he pulled his pack from the car and slung it over his shoulder. He shuffled up a steep paved drive as a vast estate came into view through a tunnel of trees. He crouched next to a pile of snow that was cleared from the driveway and surveyed the layout. No lights were visible from inside of the house. Only the porch light burned.

The four-car garage was buttoned up tight. No way to see if the BMW was home. Then he saw it. Perched atop the highest peak of the house like the gargoyle it was. The thing that attacked him in the hospital parking lot. It crouched, carefully surveying the surroundings in methodical sweeps of its gaze.

"I hate that thing," he said, as he leaned back into the snowbank. He glanced around, unsure what to do, having already reached the end of his 'big plan.' It was a good twenty-five feet of open space between him and the porch. The evergreens that offered him cover were cut back away from the house on all sides. He spied a good size opening through the tree branches next to him. He fashioned a densely packed snow ball and hurled it through the opening with all of his might. Only, it didn't sail cleanly through the opening but hit the closest branch with a loud crack and a cascade of snow toppled onto him.

"Oh crap," he said, as he dove back behind the snow bank. He lay completely still and listened for any sound indicating that the thing had heard him. He waited and waited some more, too terrified to move even a finger. The cold night air and icy snow sucked the warmth from his body, but still he refused to move. Every muscle tensed with anticipation of those razor claws tearing into his flesh or the breaking apart his bones with an unholy rage.

Nothing came. No violent jolt. No searing pain.

Finally he gained enough courage to raise his gaze. Seeing only the snow bank, he rose to his feet to peek over the bank. He found the demon's face glaring back at him only inches away. Before he could react, the demon grabbed a fist full of parka and flung him, like a rag doll, into the middle of the clearing. Bilbo landed face first and skidded across the hard-frozen lawn. The glasses fell off as he rolled onto his back and fumbled for the pocket of his suit. The demon was on him with two powerful pumps of its massive wings. Bilbo had grasped the grip of the shotgun and worked it out of the pocket when its hand pinned his arm to the ground. A sneer came across its human-like face as its black eyes peered down at him. Bilbo shoved his free hand into his other pocket and fumbled for some kind of weapon as the thing bore very inhuman like fangs. Hot drool dripped onto his quickly turned away face as his hand grasped hold of something in his pocket. He pulled out a small Gideon's New Testament. His fingers fumbled for control of it as he realized what he had. He thrust it towards the creature's face and with his most authoritative biblical voice said, "In the name of Jesus Christ, depart from me!"

Instantly the Demon let go of him and reared back. It let out a horrible shriek. Talon like claws tore at the ground bringing up chunks of frozen grass, soil and snow. It flung them into the air in a fit of rage, and then it stomped and pounded the ground with its fists.

Bilbo scuttled away and shakily climbed to his feet as he held the tiny bible out in front of him.

"Depart from me, in the name of Jesus Christ!" he continued, with more vigor.

The demon let out another long shriek toward him, then turned and sprang into the air. Its large wings pumping it into the night sky.

"Alright then," he said, as he straightened his torn parka. He put the bible back into his pocket then realized the shotgun was hanging from its lanyard at his side. He put that back in the other pocket. He then kicked around in the snow until he located his glasses. They were caked with snow but still in one piece. He decided it was too cold to put them back on and after three tries, got them into his pocket as well.

After retrieving his pack, he walked on to the house. It stood dark and silent. Only the porch light burned. Either no one was home or they were deaf, he thought. Or, they were watching him in silence. He causelessly stepped onto the porch and tried to look through the window. The blinds were drawn. He reached for the doorknob and turned it. The door opened. Guess there's no need for security when you have your very own guard demon, he reasoned. The door swung open to darkness. He leaned into the doorway and looked around, and then pulled back and opened his pack. After rummaging, he withdrew his circus flash light. He clicked it on illuminating the plastic lion's head with a strong beam of light. The large room was a picture from modern decor magazine. The furnishings were modern and precisely placed. As he stepped into the room, he let the beam pan across every inch of the room, tensing with the fear that he would find someone lurking in the shadows.

No one. Confident that he was alone, he moved to the heart of the room. He turned on his heel and peered out a large wall of windows. The view was magnificent. The kind someone with money builds a house on Lookout Mountain for. The lights of the city of Denver spread out below like a gleaming treasure chest of jewels. But its dark over lord still stood over it, staring up at him. A shiver overtook him, so he turned away.

Well, he was here but how the heck could he find it? Where would one hide the stolen soul of a person? He moved through the room. He came to a staircase and let his light probe the upper landing half, expecting to see a sinister face leering down at him. Thankfully, only stairs and ceiling were visible.

Better be systematic; one floor at a time, he thought.

The next room was a dining room. It was filled with a large dining table. It was highly polished wood, complete with tall slender candles ready for an atmospheric dinner. Strangely, it looked antique far different from the ultra modern furniture that he had encountered. Moving on, he pushed through a door into a vast kitchen with stainless steel appliances and every little thing a cook could imagine. He opened a couple of cabinets and shined his flashlight into them. He shrugged and closed them. Maybe he should chance turning on a light. It didn't seem like there was anyone here. He moved to the end of the room and flicked on a switch. The room flooded with soft light. He looked over the room and scratched his chin. The makeup was starting to get to him.

There was a door to his left and one to the right. He moved right and pushed open the door. His heart leaped to his throat. The door opened to the garage. The doctor's BMW sat in front of him, and the other stalls were filled as well. The doctor was home. He patted the shotgun in his pocket, happy to feel it. He shifted the weight of his pack on his back and gently pulled the door close.

The other door creaked open as the door to the garage closed. He turned to see the door was open about an inch.

He gripped the butt of the shotgun in his pocket and moved to the door. It pushed open and he cringed at the squeak of its hinges. It swung open to a darkened descending stairwell. A faint red and blue light reflected off of the polished floor below. He drew in a deep breath and took one step at a time, careful of his oversized shoes. The stairs ended in a large basement that was an expansive game room. It housed an elegant pool table, a bumper pool table, air hockey, and a fine mahogany bar.

The light came from a vampire themed pinball machine. Very funny, he thought.

He leaned against the pool table. His white gloved finger ran across the green felt until he came in contact with a ball. He picked it up and looked at it. The 8 ball.

"Figures," he said.

"Good evening!" came a voice.

A high-pitched squeal escaped his frame as the 8-ball dropped to the floor and rolled across the floor, where it stopped against the wall. He wheeled around, frantically searching for the source of the voice.

"Listen to them. Children of the night. What music they make." The voice spoke again.

Lights flashed on the pinball machine as Bilbo realized that the voice came from it.

He shook his head and walked over to the pool ball. He bent over to pick it up. As he gripped the ball, he was surprised to feel a slight breeze on his face. He studied the wall in front of him. His finger probed its surface. It was almost imperceptible. There was a seam running up the wall. He pushed on the wall next to the seam. It moved.

A secret doorway to a secret room. This was it. He pushed harder. The wall swung away from him. Only, there was no room beyond. It opened to a short passageway to the rock mountain on which the house was built. There was a large jagged fissure about eight feet tall and three feet wide in the rock face. He stepped up to it and looked inside. The chasm descended downward into complete blackness. His flashlight beam glared off the granite walls as he stepped into the fissure. The floor was uneven and the opening varied between four feet to about two feet in places. He slung his pack over his shoulder and proceeded deeper. His feet slid across the slick rock surface because of the awkward angle of the fissure. They wanted to become jammed in the crevice where the two sides of the rock came together. He was forced to lean on the wall as he proceeded through much of it. Soon the floor became a bit flatter but became steeper. He slipped and slid for a good fifteen to twenty minutes. He figured that he had traveled at least a mile. Still no end. But it seemed to open up ahead.

He pushed on until the passage opened up into a vast cavern. It was so vast that the beam from his flashlight could not find either the end or the ceiling of the black void. Below him, a myriad of jagged boulders cascaded downward. The thought of turning back was strong in his mind.

No! He would make a difference. He would go on.

The light scanned the boulders. They could be maneuvered over. In fact, many showed scuff marks and signs of being traveled over. And judging by the first leap, apparently by someone more agile than he.

He crouched and then sprang for the next boulder, landing on its spread eagle, grasping it with all four appendages. He then climbed to his feet and let the flashlight beam pick the next target. The next few steps were much easier to manage. In fact, things were going quite well for some time until a stone he landed on shifted under his weight, causing him to flail desperately for balance. The hand holding the light impacted a near massive rock face, forcing it from his grip. The light fell to his feet and exsanguinated upon impact. He heard its pieces clack into the stones below. He now stood in total blackness.

He clung to the large rock, too afraid to move. The blackness was complete. In fact, it was heavy, oppressive. It pressed all hope from him. His breathing became frenzied, as fear wrapped him in the darkness. He soon became light headed. He dropped to his knees, knowing he would soon pass out if he couldn't control his breathing

"Calm down" he said aloud, between gasps.

"Calm" It slowed.

"Clam" It slowed some more.

"Okay," he told himself, "Okay."

On all fours, he clung to the rock below him. He just needed to find the flashlight and everything would be alright. It shouldn't be far. He probed the stone and found its edge. He reached down between the stones to his right. He felt nothing but rock as far as he could reach. He shifted to the left side and probed until he found an opening. He stretched downward until he felt something—something a bit softer than stone. His hand ran across its surface as he tried to reason what it could be. Then it moved. Slithered actuality, under his touch. A shrill scream escaped him as he jerked his hand and his breathing instantly became frenzied again.

He tried to calm himself again, but was at a loss as to what to do.

So he prayed, "Lord what should I do?"

Then it came to him.

Put on the glasses.

He fumbled in his pocket and pulled them out. Everything became visible, like it was bathed in soft even light. He could see the entire rock slope before him. It was littered with black serpents that slithered in and out of the crevices between the stones.

Something caught his eye. The main part of the flashlight was resting in the crevice of a rock. He was able reach it, the Lion's head, and one of the batteries. When the head of a snake pushed up between the rocks, he jerked back his hand with disgust and leaped to a safer perch. After putting some more distance between him and the snake, he took in the entire cavern. It was enormous. He figured that two, maybe three Super Domes could easily fit inside it.

The rubble gave way to a large, mostly flat slab of stones that was the floor of the cavern. It looked like it had fallen from the ceiling. There were no stalactites or other cave type formations. This was all cold hard granite. But that was not the strangest thing about this cavern. Out in the middle of that flat plane stood a building, and not just any building, this one resembled a church. Complete with steeple. Only, this one was painted a dingy black and instead of the holy symbol of the cross at the top of the steeple, there stood a pentagram. Its inverted point pointing downward towards Hell.

"I'm guessing that's where I need to go," he sighed to himself as he repositioned the pack on his back.

The building loomed before him like a dark specter as he approached. His stomach burned with nervous dread as he marched toward it. The distance was farther than it first appeared. Finally, at the first step, he paused to look around. There was nothing. No movement no sound— only the heaving of his chest and the pounding of his heart. He stepped onto the first stair. The old wood creaked under his weight. Five more equally noisy steps brought him to the two doors of the entrance. The door knob looked an ancient tarnished brass.

How long had this been here? He wondered.

He gripped the knob and turned it. It turned easily and the door creaked open. It revealed a small entryway that lead to a second set of doors. Kind of like a mud room, he reasoned. After stepping through, he was surprised at the sound of the door shutting behind him. Foul, dank air seemed to fill the space in which he stood like some kind of hellish air lock. Then a sudden feeling of hopelessness washed over him. He dropped to his knees, wracked in a mournful isolation. He felt completely and utterly alone. A more desolate loneliness he had never experienced. Sobs escaped in convolutions from his body. His mind latched onto his last thought holding fast to it to keep it from being dragged into the deep sea of desperate aloneness. He blinked back the welling tears and grasped the second door knob. The door pushed open.

The place was dark. Even with the glasses. But he could make out a huge dome shaped rock protruding through the floor at the end of the room. Upon the rock stood a stone altar. He approached it and realized it was covered with small containers. As he climbed the slope of the rock, he recognized the bottles as being the same that were used to hold Beth's soul. There must have been over a hundred across the surface of the altar. His body drooped as he realized that these bottles did not contain the brilliant fluid light that he witnessed, but now contained an inky black liquid.

"Bilbo."

He wheeled at the sound of his name.

There stood the doctor in full grayish vampire glory at the base of the rock. He wore only black slacks. His pale chest was covered with various satanic tattoos and piercings. His black eyes bored into his soul.

"How does such a simpleton keep causing me so much trouble?" The doctor smiled, flashing gleaming fangs.

"What's happened to the souls?" he demanded, as he gripped the gun in his pocket.

"You really do care about them," the possessed man said, as he began to pace around the base of the rock outcropping.

"Of course I do," Bilbo answered, as he kept facing him.

"Oh, don't worry," it responded, "They are still as pure as the driven snow. For they have all been harvested before they reached the age of accountability."

"The what now?" Bilbo's thumb pulled back the hammers on the gun in his pocket.

"Your God..." the vampire raised its arms and made the quotation marks with his fingers, "...refuses to play fair. All souls remain pure until they reach an age when the can decide for themselves just whom they will serve."

"Then why are they not light?" Bilbo asked, as he shifted to keep facing his adversary.

"Ah," a vile grin crossed its face as it continued to circle the rock, "You, my friend, are in a very special place. A place that has taken me many decades to complete. This building I fashioned with painstaking consideration. Much of the wood I procured from Jonestown Guyana, the remains of Jim Jones compound. Planking and roofing was smuggled from Auchswitz concentration camp." He pointed to the ceiling. "Some of those beams are the very gallows used to hang Tom Horn. I have materials form bordellos, abortion clinics, and any unholy place that I could conceive of."

"You did this just to torture children's souls?" Bilbo asked.

The vampire stopped. "Nothing is as sweet as the suffering of the innocent." He savored. "But no. The other very special thing about this place is the stone on which you stand."

Bilbo Glanced down at the rock under his feet, unable to understand.

"It is the capstone, or lock, if you will, to a vast prison. Placed there by your God himself," he expounded. "Below are the fathers of the Nephilim."

The name was familiar to Bilbo but he could not place it. Something that God had placed in mystery.

"A race of giants so vile that God saw fit to destroy them, among other things, with the waters of the flood. The fathers of the Nephilim are creatures with such intellect and power that they are known as 'The Sons of God.'"

Bilbo's grip tightened on the stock of his weapon as the vampire resumed his pace around the rock.

"Can you imagine how grateful they would be, after being locked in darkness for over ten thousand years, to be freed into a world full of human sheep?" It looked for a response from Bilbo but found none, "I can. The only problem…" He nodded toward the altar that descended into the rock. "This lock that your God placed on this prison. You see, only something pure can work this lock."

"I guess that counts you out," Bilbo replied.

"Indeed. Indeed, it does," it agreed, as it reached out its hand. "But this should finally make it happen." Its hand opened palm up to reveal another tiny vial like the many that covered the altar.

Bilbo pulled the gun and pointed it squarely at his chest. He squeezed the trigger until it barked viciously in his grip. The first barrel of goose shot rippled across its chest just as if he shot the surface of a still pond. To his amazement, the wound dissipated and faded away in like manner.

Laughter filled the room as it stepped up onto the rock. "Bilbo, you are getting so ballsy."

Bilbo could only stand astonished.

"No matter. You see what God has kept pure before the age of accountability; I can use to open the gateway."

Bilbo shoved his hand into his pocket and found the Gideon bible. He pulled it out and sprang towards it and pressed it against the pale chest. "With the authority of Jesus Christ, I cast you out of this man."

"You do, do you?" The evil grin widened as it grasped the book at his chest and pulled it from his hand. He thrust it in Bilbo's face and let the pages fan in front of him.

Bilbo gasped, *no it couldn't be.* The vampire slapped it into his hand. He frantically opened it up and examined the page. It was blank, and so was the next one and the next. He flipped the cover. No gold script Holy Bible. Only black texture.

"I told you this was a special place." He glared down at Bilbo. "It's the only place on earth where God is not present."

It lashed out with demonic power and back handed Bilbo, sending him hurtling off the stone and skidding across the floor.

His senses slowly came back. He saw it place the vial upon the altar. It gripped the sides of it and, with all of its superhuman strength, began to twist it. Groggily, he glanced around. He saw the black book where it fell from his grip. He grabbed it, and then sat up. The backpack was still partially slung around his arm. He fumbled with the zipper until he got it open.

The demon rotated the altar until it suddenly stopped. A massive shudder rippled through the cavern. Then the altar began to sink into the stone on which it stood.

Bilbo climbed to his feet in time to see the altar complete its decent. The cavern was then filled with the sound of a horn blast. Louder, deeper, and longer than the mightiest fog horn he had ever heard. Then the earth shook violently and dust fell from the rafters.

The Vampire raised its arms in victory, tilted back its head, and shut its eyes to savor the moment.

Bilbo gathered up the shotgun at the end of its tether and pulled back the hammer on the remaining cylinder. He pointed it at the ceiling and pulled the trigger. Buckshot tore through the roof. Instantly, the vials on the altar gleamed brilliantly. He looked at the book in his hand. Once again it read Holy Bible. He dashed to his adversary and pressed the bible against it. It yelped in pain and surprise.

"Demon of Vampirism, I command you to leave this man, in the name of Jesus Christ!"

The vampire dropped to its knees as a strange growl came from the back of its throat. Bilbo kept the bible pressed against it. It tried to reach for him but as he pressed hard, its arms fell to its sides.

"Leave this man in the name of Jesus Christ!" he repeated.

It fell onto its back and began to convulse. Its arms and legs began flailing, its head thrusting from side to side. Its entire frame began to hop off the floor. The flailing and convulsing grew faster and faster until it reached impossible speeds. Soon he began to see two forms in the movement as the demon separated from its host. Then pulled itself from the now lifeless body of the doctor. Its thin bony body crab walked on its back away from the body and the bible. Grasping the bible, Bilbo lurched after it. It hissed at him through gaunt skull-like features and bared its fangs. Bilbo tossed the bible onto its chest where it landed like it was made of lead. It howled and screeched as it tried to push it off its body. It was helpless to move it.

Bilbo removed a section of broom handle that he had sharpened into a stake from his pack. He then removed his clown hammer. He stepped up to the creature and pressed the point of the stake into its chest above the heart. It snarled and grasped at the stake. Bilbo easily brushed away its arms. It had no power in the presence of God's word. He raised the hammer high and brought it down with all of his might. It made a squeak sound as the two-pound sledge drove the stake into its chest. Again, and again it squeaked until the stake ran through its body and into the floor.

Bilbo rose and retrieved his Bible as the demon writhed and clawed, unable to free itself. The deep bellow of the horn sounded again as he looked at the lifeless body of Doctor Marnau. The body was shriveled, with deep creases in his face—the way a hundred and thirty-year-old body should, without the benefit of an immortal being within it.

"Don't leave me like this!" The demon cried out as it desperately tried to free itself from where it had been pegged.

Bilbo tossed the hammer aside and moved to the gleaming bottles on the altar.

"Beth?" he called. "Beth, can you hear me?"

One of the bottles seemed to blink as he called out her name. He carefully plucked the tiny bottle from the others. He grasped it tightly, and then held it against his chest. "Thank you, Lord." He opened his palm before him. "I'm going to get you home."

He glanced up at the other bottles. He placed Beth's vial into his pocket. He then emptied his pack and stuffed the others in it.

The horn blasted again, long and deep.

"Don't leave me," the demon called again, "I swear that I will never hurt you. I will disappear into the darkness, forever."

Bilbo glanced back and watched it try and pull the stake from its chest. But the stake severed its source of power for as long as it remained.

"I think it's better if you stick around here." He carefully secured the pack onto his back and headed for the door.

Outside the building, he scampered down the steps. The mighty horn sounded again, reverberating through the cavern. That's when he saw the three large passageways had opened up in the walls of the cavern. They were at least twenty feet tall and about as wide. He could tell that they quickly descended in steep slopes. He thought about going for a better look but he could hear something from its depths. Something ascending with urgency and fury.

Bilbo made the best time possible across the distance from the building to the rock incline. It had become alive with the shiny black serpents. He clutched his Bible then patted the vial in his pocket and climbed onto the rocks. He chose his path carefully, having to step over and around the slithering creatures. The serpents were so numerous that he had a hard time finding footholds. A queasiness overcame him as the foul-smelling things were actually oozing a dark slime.

"He guides me in paths of righteousness for His name's sake..." He started to recite Psalm 23, surprised how easily he could recollect it. His next step slipped on the slime covered stone and landed on top of a particularly thick serpentine body. Its wide dark head rose and curled around to face him at about eye level.

"Even though I walk through the valley of the ..." His voice began to waver as the forked tongue flicked in front of his face. "...shadow of death,..."

Its glassy eyes seemed to probe his every feature.

" I will fear no evil..." The last word squeaked out weekly.

The thing began to coil as if poised to strike. He gripped his bible and pushed it out in front of his face.

"Your rod and Your staff they comfort me."

The snake seemed to lose interest, lowered its head and slithered away.

"You prepare a table before me in the presence of my enemies." He exhaled long and hard as that horrible horn sounded again. He looked back. Dark smoke was now pouring from the passageways.

When he reached the summit of his climb, he paused before entering the passageway and looked back. The cavern was almost filled with thick black smoke. But even through the smoke he could see a red glow from the three newly open doorways. He could also see something moving in the churning smoke. Something dark and sinister.

He made much better time going through the fissure—even with the extra care he gave his precious cargo. The massive horn could still be heard even as he entered the basement of the house. He paused and looked at the doorway. He had to do something to seal it. He couldn't let what was in there get out.

He ran up the stairs as fast as his big red shoes would let him. He frantically moved through the house scanning every inch of it. He needed something. Something he prayed the Lord would show him. That's when he saw the large sliding glass door. It opened onto a huge deck that led down to an elegantly lighted landscape. With a head like it was mounted on a swivel, he surveyed the yard.

There, built into flagstone and rock, an outdoor kitchen. He pulled open the doors under a stainless-steel Bar B-Q. He unscrewed the line on a propane tank and pulled it free. In the house he hustled through the dining, room swiping the two candles from the table as he passed.

He made it back to the basement in time to hear the horn sound again. The smoke began to creep from the fissure as he arrived. At about ten feet into the opening, he shoved the tank into the crevice where the walls came together at the floor. After locating a shot gun shell in his pocket, he wedged it between the tanks valve and the protective collar—the business end facing the valve. Under it, he placed the candles horizontally, side by side, the wick at opposing sides. If this worked, the candle should burn down to the shell, set it off, blow the tank, and hopefully give him time to escape. He lit the candles. The wax poured away much quicker in their inverted position than he expected. Beth's bottle was safe in the pocket he checked as he grabbed up the pack and beat it out of there.

Vapor wafted off of his head and his breath geysered from his mouth in the cold air as he made it to the clown car. He looked back to the house. It sat still and quiet. Maybe it didn't work. He gently placed the pack into the car when the house burst forth with glass, wood, and flame. The concussion knocked Bilbo to the frozen ground. He used the car to climb to his feet as he pulled the bottle from his pocket. It was intact and glowed brightly. He climbed into the tiny car and it roared to life.

Did the explosion seal the cavern? He had no idea. He hoped so. He prayed that it did.

The bitter cold bit through the makeup as the car bound towards the city and its dark specter. The massive demon's gaze bore down on him as if it were lead. It extended its arm and unfurled its slender index finger and pointed at him. Bilbo gripped the wheel and focused on the road. Nothing would hinder his mission.

Winged demons circled overhead as he pulled into the hospital parking lot and the clawed spiders skittered menacingly on the asphalt in vast numbers. He exited the car and with a firm grip on Beth's vial, he kicked the spider creatures out of his path as they gathered to hinder his progress. Inside the building was alive with demonic creatures but he paid them no heed as he marched toward the elevator.

"Hey," a voice called out. "Hey you!"

Bilbo caught sight of the security guard out of the corner of his eye. A security guard that, no doubts, had orders not to let the trouble making Clown back into the hospital.

"Stop right there."

Bilbo made it to the elevator and pushed the button and looked up to the arrow above the door as the sound of the hard soles broke into a trot behind him.

"You in the clown get up."

With the sound of a ding, the door slid open and Bilbo stepped in and turned to face the open doorway. The guard was almost to him when he pulled the shotgun and pointed it at the ceiling. The guard slid to a stop, his hands held in a 'don't shoot me' position as the door slid shut.

When the door to the intensive care ward opened, he put away the gun. He marched out and recognized the nurse instantly. It would have to be her, he thought, but marched on toward the confrontation.

She looked at the small vial in his hand, and then into his eyes, then nodded to her right.

"She's in there."

"Thanks!" was his reply.

The guard plus two others rushed in from the stairway and immediately zeroed in on him.

"No, no." The nurse stood, holding out her arms. "It's okay. He's supposed to be here."

The men looked at each other then reluctantly turned and left.

Bilbo entered the room and slowly approached the small form squarely positioned in the bed. She had not moved in some time. He knelt down beside her and took her tiny hand in his.

"I'm sorry this has happened to you," he softly spoke, "I'm sorry I let you down."

He took the brightly glowing vial and held it close to her. He wrenched the silver lid free and placed it on her chest. For a moment it became more brilliant, and then faded to nothing.

The rhythmic rise and fall of her chest increased then became labored. She began to convulse, her eyes fluttered open but were rolled back in her head. Alarms began to sound from the equipment that was attached to her.

"Nurse!" he called, climbing to his feet.

Beth grew still and peaceful as the nurse rushed in. She set to checking readings and examining her with deliberate efficiency. She turned off the alarms and worked in silence until she finally began removing the intravenous tubing.

Bilbo could only stare as a deep hollowness filled his core. He dreaded the glance of the nurse which came directly.

"I'm sorry, she's gone," she stated, "The doctor will have to call it."

Bilbo nodded. He picked up the empty vial which had fallen to Beth's side, then turned and walked out. Even with the glasses removed he could still see the shadows of evil around him. That is, until the tears that welled blurred even that.

He shuffled into the elevator and turned to stare at the floor buttons. He pushed one. The next thing he realized, he was looking out of the open doorway. Unsure how long he had stood there, he stepped out.

He barely noticed the small form that shuffled into the dark hallway. The young boy stood in his hospital gown and looked up at him with awe. Bilbo paused, reached down, and ruffled his hair; then walked on with the boy looking at him.

Outside the night seemed colder and emptier than ever before. He made it to his car as the black 57 Chevy rolled up. The driver's window opened, revealing the elderly nun.

"You alright?" she asked.

"No."

Sympathy oozed from the sister as she studied him.

Bilbo reached into the car and withdrew the backpack full of souls. "Would you see to this?"

He handed it to her, and then climbed into his car. The engine roared to life. It backed up and he pointed it into the night.

THE PUNCHLINE.

Here is a preview of

DEMON' CARNIVAL

THE FARTHER ADVENTURES OF BILBO THE CLOWN

https://www.amazon.com/dp/B07PWNKZ9N/ref=nav_timeline_asin?_encoding=UTF8&psc=1

Your enemy the devil prowls around like a roaring lion looking for someone to devour.
1 Peter 5:8 New International Version

The bobtail Kenworth's headlights bounced as it crested the hill on an old oilfield road somewhere in north eastern Wyoming. The chrome nude silhouettes on the mud flaps gleamed in the moonlight as the rig came to rest with the sharp release of its airbrakes. The lights disappeared as the rattle of the engine fell silent. The truck sat silent as the dust settled around it like some African beast that had breathed its last. Then almost without sound, the driver's door popped open and a dark figure stepped out onto the upper step and paused to scan the area. He then turned and climbed down. He pushed the door closed. His finger reached to a sticker just under the door handle. It was another nude silhouette. This one a sexy form standing profile. It was adorned with devil's horns and spade shaped tail. He smiled as he probed its breast with his finger. He then walked around the truck his eye searching the moon lit hills of dry grass and sage brush. There was no other sign of civilization for as far as his eyes could see. He rounded to the passenger door. This one was adorned with a similar sticker only with a Halo and angel's wings. He pulled open the door and drug out two heavy trash bags form the floorboards. He lugged them a good fifty feet from the truck and let them drop at his feet. He stood silently looking and listening. He could hear only the breeze and the faint rhythmic screech of an oil derrick form somewhere over the gently rolling hills. He knelt and untied the knots in each bag. He reached in and withdrew a hunk of some kind of raw meat and tossed it out into the brittle grass. He repeated the motion until both bags were empty. He then returned to the truck and rummaged through his sleeper breath until he withdrew the game call. Which was not much more than a camouflage covered box with an electric speaker attached. He selected a setting as he returned to his bait and turned it on. The hills filled with high pitched screeches meant to mimic the cry of a distressed rabbit. As the cries filled the night he dug a small pit with a collapsible shovel. That done, he put it away and retuned with a small bundle of clothing which he tossed into the pit then soaked with a healthy stream of lighter fluid. The eruption of flame revealed eager eyes and he sat back against the wheel of his truck and watched it be consumed.

The flame had almost died away when he noticed the first movement on the hill. A skittish form slunk from behind a clump of sagebrush, its pulsing nose sampling the air. The K-9 eyes hungerly searching for the source of the cries. Soon another scrawny Coyote bounded into to view and loped towards the call. He was watching the two creatures snap up pieces of meat and chew just enough so that they could swallow when he noticed the movement from the corner of his eye. From behind the rig another Coyote emerged then stood by the rear tires. This one was by far the largest of the animals. It lifted its nose to the breeze, its nostrils flaring. It either didn't notice the stone still human or it just didn't care as it stared toward to call. Seeing the other coyotes, the hackles on its mangy fur raised and it bolted toward them. The other animals gulped what they could then cowered and slunk back as the larger animal approached. It chose a large piece of meat and then returned back toward the truck.

The man sat perfectly still as the creature came almost directly at him. He smiled as it trotted by with its new-found dinner in its jaws. He could see it clearly in the moon light. In fact, he could even make out the bright green fingernail polish at the end of the stiffened fingers as it passed by. His gaze followed it until it disappeared into the shadows. Still grinning he laid his head back against the tire and closed his eyes.

Bilbo the Clown clutched the large carpet bag as he patiently paced the old nun down the corridor. His makeup was fresh. The big blue frown in place. His red and white suit freshly laundered. As much as he hated this part he would at least look tip top.

"It's this one," The frail slightly hunch backed Sister Sledge pointed to a door at the end of the corridor.

He never understood how but she managed to locate most of Dr. Murnau's innocent victims. This one was at Ivinson Memorial Hospital in Laramie Wyoming. They pushed through the door into a darkened room. Bilbo studied the small boy made even smaller by the machines that kept his body alive. Such a sweet face desecrated with tubes.

He sat down the bag as the sister made the sign of the cross and began to pray. He opened it to find the brilliant light cast form the tiny bottles. There were only a few left. One gleamed brighter than the others. He reached in and gently withdrew it. He approached the bed and stood over the child. Thoughts of Beth taking her last breath, flooded his mind again. Her and every other child he had returned their souls to. Damn, he hated this part.

The sister nodded her encouragement. He held out the bottle and twisted off the cap. The light grew incredibly intense as he sat it on the boy's chest. His tiny body began to convulse and strain in the neatly tucked blanket. Bilbo turned his head. He did not want to see another child die. Then he saw something out of the corner of his eye. The boy's eyes had opened. He gasped as tears filled his eyes. He reached down and took the boy's hand.

"It's going to be alright," he beamed. "Everything is going to be alright."

The tiny frame twisted with displeasure as he began to gag on the breathing tube. Bilbo reached to remove the tube then paused unsure of just how to go about it. He looked at the Nun for answers.

"Go get a nurse," she ordered.

His body Jerked into action. "Yes, yes a nurse." He dashed out the door and turned to his left. He took a few paces before he realized he was going the wrong way. "I'm getting a nurse," he called the nun as he passed back by the door. She shook her head and retuned to consoling the boy.

The electric blue Kenworth led the line of trucks down the side streets of Broomfield Colorado. A large mural that read "Ride the Shocker," spanned the length of the trailer. Sean pulled the shade down to block the afternoon glare. Tattoos of voluptuous women covered his bear arms to about cuff length at his wrist. His gaze was instantly drawn to the girls, all in their short shorts strutting down the side walk. These were young. But then he liked them young. He glanced up and took note of the sign that read Westview Community Church. It was a neat light-colored building with a cross on a small steeple, nestled in a quiet little neighborhood. He stared at them as he passed. The blond in the middle looked at him realizing his desire. She tossed back her hair with exaggerated motion then blew him a kiss as the other girls laughed and waved.

Such a tease. He thought. Now she could be quite a treat.

Rick Jefferson shuffled through the paper in his neat but small desk. He knew that he had seen the insert from the party store in the paper. It was his task to plan the summer jamboree. And since he was newly appointed as a youth pastor, he didn't want to disappoint. The trick would be to make something that would appeal to both the teens and the younger children since the smaller size of the church dictated combining both groups. His eyes fell on an advertisement for some swimwear. A curvy blond woman posed seductively across the page. His eyes followed the curves of her body. His thoughts turned to…

"No!" he threw it into the waste basket. "Not this time." He stood up and paced around the room. He hated it. The power his eyes had over him. He moved to the window and looked out. He saw the three girls and shook his head. He recognized them instantly as they strutted barely dressed down the sidewalk. JJ was the leader of the group. He had tried to reach her for some time but she was having none of it. She seemed hell bent on the wrong path. She was an early bloomer and quite attractive looking. She looked much older than her fourteen years. She had come to realize the power her looks had over the boys but had no idea of the dangers. And for the time being she was part of the youth group as mandated by her mother Janis. He didn't know if it was a blessing or a curse, but he would do the work that God put before him. He glanced at his watch.

Must be time to start.

2

Sean rolled down the sleeves of his shirt to cover the tattoos as he saw the man get out of the Red Camry. He knew instantly who he was. He had to deal with one of these pain in the ass city or county safety inspectors in every town he set up in. It wasn't the ride that caused the trouble. It was just a basic octopus ride. No, it was the show that they hated. The spectacle that made his The Shocker the star attraction of South Star Amusements. The design was his own. Tree eight-foot-tall glass monoliths placed around the perimeter of the ride. They housed a V-shaped industrial gage wire that ascended from the bottom of the case. When turned on a magnificent arc of electricity that traveled, crackling up the V making it the largest Jacobs ladders he knew of. The ride itself was outfitted with blue lights that ran along the arms of the octopus that extended from a large center pillar. Atop of this pillar was fashioned a large plasma globe, almost four feet in diameter. When turned on brilliant blue and red bolts of electricity probed the walls of the globe from a round topped post in it center. The effect was stunning.

The balding man approached hitching up his pants over a flabby belly. His gaze glued to the glass cases. Sean extended his hand. "Good morning."

"I hear we have something special here," the man said ignoring Sean's hand.

"I like to think so," Sean answered. His fingers went to his earlobe and probed the gauge in it, the way he always did when he got irritated.

The inspector leaned over and peered at the connections at the base of the case. "This if highly irregular."

"I assure you it's been approved by multiple agencies. I have got plenty of paperwork here you can look at. Mr.......?"

"Keagan," he said without looking up. "City of Broomfield." He tapped the glass with his finger. "Yes, highly irregular."

Sean strolled to the back of his open trailer. He grabbed a six-foot long pole. It had a Metal point on the end and a small hook. He used it form many things like pulling down the rear door when the strap was caught up or pulling things just out of reach. His grip tightened on it as he watched Mr. Keagan shake his head as he inspected the cables leading to he displays. He then turned and inserted the point into a metal ring protruding from a canvas pouch fastened to the trailer wall. He pushed upward and lifted a packet of bound pages from the pouch. He lowered it and grasped the packet then turned to the inspector.

"You should find all of the proper certifications in here," he said and handed it to the man.

Kegan took it without really looking at it. "This is going to take a little looking into," he smiled. No smirked really. A self-important look of superiority that so many of these ass-holes had. Just because they could. "Might take a few days." He finished.

Sean smiled back. "We open tomorrow."

Keagan shrugged, the smile still across his face. "Can't make any promises."

"I'm sure you'll do your best," Sean answered. He figured a fifty-dollar bill might fix the situation as it almost always did, but he just didn't feel like playing today. He turned and walked off. 'I'll catch you later then."

Keagan watched him walk off a bit surprised. He shook his head and headed back to his Camry.

William rubbed his shoulder as he trudged to the timeclock and punched in his employee number. A task that seemed harder to do every day. He knew he was lucky to have a job. He had been getting pretty desperate when he came to Harmon Farms. It was the fifth largest poultry producer in the country. A fact that his manager, Jim Bishop, reminded them of often. The job wasn't that hard, It did not take a brain surgeon to do it, but he still felt frustrated that he could never seem to master it, never seemed that he could keep up. The mostly Hispanic workforce appeared to resent him. He was always an outsider.

Today's task was his least favorite. It was his job to remove the chickens from their tiny cages as wheeled rack after wheeled rack was pushed in. He would then hang the flapping birds by their strapped feet on a passing conveyor hook. He would then stick two electric prods to their bodies that sent a paralyzing charge through them. The chickens would stretch their necks toward the ground as they were carried between v-shaped pipes that funneled their necks into a sharp blade. They would bleed out as they entered a machine that ran spinning, fingered rubber balls against them that would strip the feathers from their bodies. Once out of the machine, other workers would cut them open and reach in and pull the internal organs out. It was when one of the chickens didn't get sufficiently stunned and missed the blade, that sent him into a panicked rush to get his knife and cut its throat before the poor thing entered the machine alive and aware.

William smiled as he saw Manny, a Hispanic man in his early twenties enter. He was one of the few people there that was friendly to him. Manny smiled at him then grimaced as he tried to put on his gloves.

"You alright?" William asked.

The man nodded and forced a smile. "Is okay," he responded in broken English.

William walked over to him. He could see the man's hands were swollen to twice their normal size. He realized why Manny was working with him today and not on the other side of the wall were he usually worked. There the task of gutting the birds required repeated manipulation of the hand into the birds. A task he himself did until it was deemed, he couldn't keep up with production and moved here.

He gently took the man's hand and looked him in the eyes. "You need to get this looked at."

"No, no. Is okay," he smiled and forced the glove on. "Is Okay. See."

The alarm sounded, and the conveyer started with a jolt. Time to go to work. He took the first bird from its cage, looked at its wondering eyes. Eyes he could truly identify with. Eyes that could see but had no understanding of its part in the prosses. A prosses designed to use and destroy. For someone else's benefit.

William shuffled into the house, after pulling another double shift. He rubbed the aching spot between his neck and shoulder. That familiar, hollow, hopeless feeling taking dominion of his existence. Like warm fingers slowly constricting around his neck. He sat on his couch and stared at the darkened television for some time but did not turn it on. How had he arrived here? He pondered. Existing merely to exist. Like a cog in a machine of desperation.

How could he continue like this?

He couldn't, he realized. He couldn't continue like this.

He then noticed the package of balloons and syringe type inflator that he had left on the coffee table. He almost laughed.

His dream. His stupid little Clown dream. All that he had left. He leaned forward and looked at the book next to it. 'How to make a living out of balloon animals.' He realized how stupid it sounded. How if he were to say the words, I am a clown out loud it would sound absurd. Pathetic.

Yet people did it. People did things in their lives that they dreamed of doing. People did things that allowed them to enjoy their lives. To not dread each day. To not wish their lives away.

He picked up the book. What if he failed at this too? Like he had failed so many times before.

He knew he would not be able of bear it. But what if he did not try?

He selected an entry from the book and set to work blowing up a balloon. He carefully followed each step as he manipulated the balloon. Checking some steps multiple times. Soon a shape began to form. He smiled. One more step and he would have it. He would have a ... Pop! The creation became a limp fragment in his hands.

Steve Keagan wobbled just a bit as he stepped from the elevator into the parking garage. Probably should not have had that last drink. He strolled out trying to remember where he parked the Camry. The parking structure was now much more open with far fewer cars than when he arrived. He had to park on the third level of the four-level parking structure. He always hated driving in these confined spaces. His footstep echoed off the walls in the still warm night air when another sound overtook it. Laughter. A strange kind of giggle that sent a shiver across his flesh. Something about it was not quite right. It had a ring of lunacy to it.

He could see his Camry when he noticed something else. A man, no a clown kneeling in the middle of the isle. He was staring down at something and giggling. It was a small rodent that had gotten flattened by a car. As he slowed to a stop the clown looked up at him. This clown had a bright blue Mohawk and wore a blue and white suit. Its face had Blue lightning bolts that crossed its eyes and met at its nose. Below that a large blue Cheshire cat grin that curled in on itself at the corners gave it a most sinister look. The clown laughed out loud as he stood.

Thank you so much for reading Bilbo the Clown Fights Evil. It is humbling to know someone has taken the time to read my work. I hope you enjoyed it. I would love to here form you. People who leave reviews are a true asset to us writers in many ways. Even the not so positive reviews. I would sure love it if you took a moment to leave one. Even it its just a word or two.

https://www.amazon.com/gp/product/B01M0DFP1I/ref =dbs_a_def_rwt_bibl_vppi_i0

You can also visit: http://bilbotheclown.com/

Art word by Jordan Harris

Made in the USA
Middletown, DE
22 April 2021